The Berenstain Bears GO TO CAMP

A FIRST TIME BOOK®

CAMP

The Berenstain Bears GO

 Published in the United States by Random House, Inc., New York, and simultaneously in Canada by Random House of Canada Limited, Toronto. *Library of Congress Cataloging in Publication Data:* Berenstain, Stan, 1923– . The Berenstain bears go to camp. (Berenstain bears first time books) SUMMARY: The Berenstain cubs enjoy day camp, although they are dubious about the end-of-season powwow and sleep-out at the top of Skull Rock. [1. Camping—Fiction. 2. Bears—Fiction] I. Berenstain, Jan, 1923– . II. Title. III. Series: Berenstain, Stan, 1923– . Berenstain bears first time books. PZ7.B4483Bep [E] 81-15864 AACR2 ISBN: 0-394-85131-5 (trade); 0-394-95131-X (lib. bdg.) Manufactured in the United States of America

39 40

NEWS
TO CAMP
Stan and Jan Berenstain
RANDOM HOUSE • NEW YORK

The Bear Country SCHOOL

It was the last day of school and the beginning of vacation—that wonderful time when little bears could sit around doing absolutely nothing. Brother Bear and Sister Bear shouted good-bye to Teacher Jane and hopped onto the bus for the happy trip home.

"Well?" asked Mama Bear after a day or so of vacation. "Are you enjoying sitting around doing nothing?"

"It's great!" said Sister.

"Absolutely!" said Brother.

"There's just one trouble with it," added Sister. *"There's nothing to do!"*

"Here, take a look at this," said Mama as she reached for something that had come in the mail.

This is what it looked like:

Some of the things looked interesting. But Brother wondered what "fully supervised" meant. And Sister wasn't so sure about that "overnight sleep-out." It sounded a little scary.

"Where is this camp?" asked Sister.
"Not far," answered Mama.
"How will we get there?" Brother wanted to know.
"A bus comes for you in the morning and brings you home in the afternoon."
"Sounds a little like school," said Brother.
"We'll think about it," said the cubs, and went back to doing nothing—well, not exactly nothing. . . .

They picked a few wildflowers,

chased a few butterflies,

turned over a few rocks . . .

—and thought about it.

"Mama, could we try Grizzly Bob's Day Camp just to see if we like it?" they asked.

"Of course," said Mama.

A couple of mornings later, Brother and Sister were in camp shorts and T-shirts, all ready and waiting when the bus came.

It didn't look much like the school bus.

And Grizzly Bob
didn't look much like Teacher Jane.

And the camp didn't look
anything like school!

Grizzly Bob had built his camp beside a lake at the edge of the forest. There were log buildings, a flagpole flying the camp flag, a big bulletin board with the camp rules—there certainly were a lot of rules—some interesting paths, a roped-in place to swim. . . . There was even a big red canoe!

ARTS AND CRAFTS
OFFICE
BOB
CAMP RULES

Bob had made name tags for the cubs. "You're campmates now, so you better get to know each other," he said.

Then he took them on a tour of the camp. There was an office with a desk, where he did his paperwork, and a first-aid corner full of bandages and things for cuts and bruises.

There was a Rec Hall to go into when it rained. "Rec" was short for recreation.

There was a picnic place and a barbecue pit where they roasted hot dogs for lunch. Sister burned hers a little, but she traded with another cub who liked burned hot dogs.

Bob announced that after lunch they would all climb up Spook Hill to the very top of Skull Rock—the special place where they would have their end-of-camp powwow and sleep-out.

It was quite a climb!

That evening Mama and Papa Bear were eager to know how the cubs liked camp.

"It was okay," said Brother. "But they sure have a lot of rules!"

"It was all right," agreed Sister. "They sure have plenty of bandages and stingy stuff for cuts!"

But what they were both thinking about was Skull Rock and that end-of-camp sleep-out.

Especially Sister.

The second day was different. Brother had a great day. He passed the swimming test and was allowed to ride in the canoe.

Sister didn't have such a good day. She played dodge ball and some of the cubs threw pretty hard.

The third day Sister had fun. She got a star for a birch picture frame she made in arts and crafts. But Brother hurt his knee in the wheelbarrow race.

The fourth day both
of them had fun—

And every day after that! So much fun that they forgot about Skull Rock and the sleep-out . . .

—almost.

Papa found the sleeping bags that he and Mama had used on their honeymoon, and when the camp bus came on the morning of the big night, Brother and Sister were ready . . . sort of.

The climb up Spook Hill wasn't so hard this time—even with backpacks. The cubs were strong and tough from their summer of camping. Tomorrow would be Field Day—the last day of camp, when their parents would come to watch their games and contests and see awards given out. But, for now, all the cubs could think about was the big sleep-out.

It was just beginning to get dark when they reached Skull Rock.

Grizzly Bob built a campfire. Then he went into a small cave. When he came out, he was dressed in a beautiful Indian costume!

Then the cubs sat in a semicircle, and the powwow began.

Bob told them old Indian legends of the great animal spirits—the story of the Great Grizzly as Big as a Mountain, the Soaring Eagle Who Filled the Sky, and the Mighty Salmon Whose Colors Made the Rainbow.

As Bob told the old stories, the cubs could almost see the wonderful creatures in the firelit smoke as it curled up into the night sky.

After the powwow, they had cocoa and honey bread. Then they curled up in their sleeping bags. And soon they were all fast asleep . . . even Sister.

The next day Brother and Sister did very well in the Field Day games and contests.

Brother won a trophy for finishing second in the dash, and Sister got medals for the dead-bear's float and for her bead belt.

It was almost the end of summer; school would be starting in a couple of weeks.

"Well?" asked Papa. "How did you like camp?"

"It was great!" said Brother, hugging his trophy.

"It was great!" agreed Sister, wearing her medals proudly. "But you know something? After Grizzly Bob's Day Camp, school will be like a vacation!"